R

MADRON∧

NO LONGER PROPERTY OF
SEATTLE PUBLIC LIBRARY

To Noah, who hugged it first—
and to Sam, who loves to see over the fence
—M.B.

In memory of John Glashan
—L.D.

Balzer + Bray is an imprint of
HarperCollins Publishers.

Raisin, the Littlest Cow
Text copyright © 2017 by Miriam Busch
Illustrations copyright © 2017 by Larry Day
All rights reserved. Manufactured in China.

No part of this book may be used or reproduced in any manner whatsoever without written permission except
in the case of brief quotations embodied in critical articles and reviews. For information address HarperCollins
Children's Books, a division of HarperCollins Publishers, 195 Broadway, New York, NY 10007.
www.harpercollinschildrens.com

ISBN 978-0-06-242763-2 (trade bdg.)

The artist used pencil, ink, gouache, and watercolor on Twinrocker handmade watercolor paper
to create the illustrations for this book.
Typography by Dana Fritts
16 17 18 19 20 SCP 10 9 8 7 6 5 4 3 2 1
❖
First Edition

RAISIN
the Littlest Cow

by **Miriam Busch**   illustrated by **Larry Day**

BALZER + BRAY
An Imprint of HarperCollins*Publishers*

Raisin was the littlest cow in the herd.
She liked it that way.

The bigger cows cooed and nuzzled
her, and on movie night, they even
helped her see over the fence.

Raisin adored movies.
She was perfectly content.

Things she didn't like:

Yuck!
Cauliflower
Bedtime
Funny Smells
Tomato Juice
Thunder
Change

Raisin absolutely did not like change.

But change came, as change does.

One Thursday, her mother had a cow . . .
one who was even smaller than Raisin.
The other cows nuzzled him. "Such a tiny
cow!" they cooed.

Raisin stomped to the fence.

She added "Thursdays" to her list.

"Raisin," called her mother, "would you like to see your brother?"

"No," said Raisin.

"Oh," said her mother, "would you like to feed your brother?"

"No," said Raisin.

"Raisin," said her mother, "what shall we name your brother?"

Raisin didn't answer. She made another list:

Places to run away to:

Timbuktu
Siberia
Jupiter

At snack time, the other cows were still busy cooing and nuzzling. "Mmmoo!" they said. "He looks just like a miniature Raisin!"

"He looks like a cauliflower," grumbled Raisin.

Her mother raised an eyebrow. "He needs a name," she said.
"Let's call him Thursday," Raisin suggested helpfully. She
wrinkled her nose. "Thursday smells funny," she said.
Her mother's tail twitched a warning twitch.
Raisin took her snack to the fence.

She waited for the movie to begin. And waited.
Surely the bigger cows would come to boost her up.
Finally, the sky darkened. Raisin smelled popcorn!

Places to
run away to:

Timbuktu
Siberia
Jupiter

If only she could see one more movie
before she took off for Jupiter tomorrow.
But where were the bigger cows?
Who would boost her up now?

Raisin knew what to do.

"I did it myself!"

GRRrUMMmm, growled the sky.
"Hush," said Raisin.
One drop of rain plopped on
Raisin's nose.
"That's nothing!" she said.
The sky disagreed.

"Stop that," cried Raisin.
The rain roared down.

"Thursday stinks," Raisin yelled, but no one heard her. They were all still too busy cooing over Raisin's replacement.

Raisin drooped. Great. She'd end up positively wrinkled, and no one would even know.

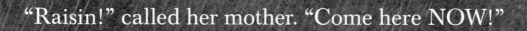

"Raisin!" called her mother. "Come here NOW!"

MOVIE CANCELED

Fine.

Raisin sloshed through mud.

Raisin did NOT like thunder.

She ran the rest of the way.

BUDUMDOOM! drummed the sky.

"Waaah!"

wailed the baby.

"Shsshh," whispered the other cows, but the baby bawled at every rumble. Raisin splished through the crowd. Raindrops trickled from her back down her legs to her hooves. Her tail dripped.

But Raisin wasn't wrinkled. "I boosted myself up today," she told them.

Raisin covered her sopping ears. "You're almost as loud as the thunder," she said.

The baby gazed at her.
Raisin couldn't help but notice:
his eyes were her favorite color.

The baby sucked in a deep breath.
But before he could wail again, Raisin
whispered, "I don't like thunder, either."

Water rolled down Raisin's snout and splashed to the
ground. One fat raindrop plopped onto the baby's head.
He almost smiled.

"Watch this," Raisin said. She shook her coat. Water flew . . .

. . . everywhere!

The baby giggled.
Raisin giggled, too.

"You really are the littlest cow," Raisin said.
She nuzzled her brother.
He cooed.

"Your name is Raindrop," Raisin
whispered. "And tomorrow, I'll help you
see over the fence."